AMULET

KAZU KIBUISHI

BOOK THREE
THE CLOUD SEARCHERS

graphix

AN IMPRINT OF

SCHOLASTIC

KRAK
KRAK

KRAK
KRAK
KRAK

KRAK
KRAK
KRAK

KRAK!
KRAK!

LUGER.

TR-TRELLIS.

HAVE YOU COME TO FINISH ME OFF?

I HAVE NO INTENTION OF KILLING YOU.

LOOK. I DESTROYED THE STONE.

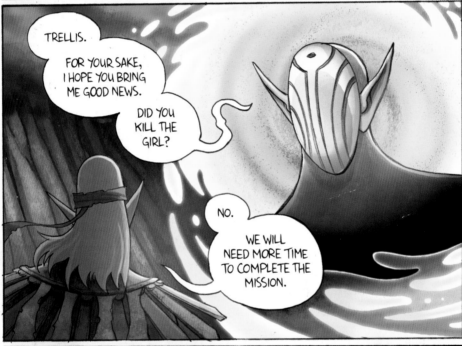

TRELLIS.

FOR YOUR SAKE, I HOPE YOU BRING ME GOOD NEWS.

DID YOU KILL THE GIRL?

NO.

WE WILL NEED MORE TIME TO COMPLETE THE MISSION.

THIS WAS YOUR LAST CHANCE.

YOU UNDERSTOOD THIS.

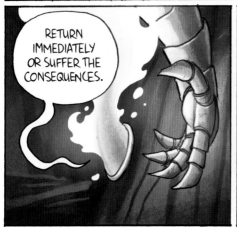

MASTER GABILAN,

THANK YOU FOR COMING ON SUCH SHORT NOTICE.

AND MAY I ADD WHAT AN HONOR IT IS TO MEET YOU.

JUST TAKE ME TO THE KING.

YES, THIS WAY.

GABILAN THE ASSASSIN IS HERE TO SEE YOU, SIRE!

WELCOME, GABILAN.

YOU HAVE BEEN INFORMED OF YOUR TARGETS?

THERE IS ONE MORE...

YES.

A YOUNG FEMALE STONE-KEEPER AND HER COMPANIONS.

PRINCE TRELLIS?

DESPITE FAIR WARNING, HE HAS CHOSEN TO BETRAY ME AGAIN.

TREASON IS PUNISHABLE BY DEATH.

YOU ASK ME TO KILL YOUR SON?

BETTER MEN HAVE FAILED, GABILAN.

SURPRISE ME.

YOUR PAYMENT, SIR.

DO YOU ENJOY WORKING FOR YOUR MASTER, DEAR LOGI?

IT IS NOT ABOUT ENJOYMENT, SIR. IT IS SIMPLY SURVIVAL.

FOR MY SERVICES, HE ALLOWS ME TO LIVE.

A MOST UNFORTUNATE ARRANGEMENT.

I PROMISE TO OFFER YOU A BETTER WAGE --

COGSLEY, THIS IS IMPOSSIBLE!

THERE'S NO WAY WE CAN HIDE IT!

WE HAVE TO TRY, MISKIT!

WE CAN'T JUST LEAVE HER OUT IN THE OPEN!

COGSLEY'S TAKING THIS PRETTY HARD.

WELL, HE DID BUILD THE HOUSE WITH SILAS.

IT'S LIKE HIS BABY.

WE'LL COME BACK FOR YOU!

SOB

WHERE'S LEON?

LAST TIME I SAW HIM, HE WAS IN SILAS'S LIBRARY.

OH, EMILY.

I'VE BEEN SEARCHING THESE BOOKS ALL MORNING AND I STILL CAN'T FIND IT.

FIND WHAT?

OUR DESTINATION. MY JOB IS TO ESCORT YOU TO THE CITY OF CIELIS.

THERE'S ONLY ONE PROBLEM.

THE CITY DISAPPEARED.

DISAPPEARED?

OR IT WAS DESTROYED. DEPENDING ON WHO YOU ASK.

THE ELF ARMY SET FIRE TO THE CITY MANY YEARS AGO.

SOME SAY ALL OF THE CITIZENS PERISHED.

BUT CAN YOU IMAGINE KILLING THE MOST POWERFUL STONEKEEPERS IN THE WORLD WITH A FIRE?

RIDICULOUS.

STONE-KEEPERS?

THEY WERE THE RULERS OF ALLEDIA BEFORE THE ELF KING CAME TO POWER.

THE LEADERS OF THIS CITY CAME TO BE KNOWN AS THE GUARDIAN COUNCIL.

THE FIVE GREAT STONEKEEPERS WHO COMPRISED THE GUARDIAN COUNCIL WERE CHOSEN TO GOVERN ALLEDIA. FOR MANY YEARS, THINGS WENT ACCORDING TO THEIR PLANS AND ALLEDIA BENEFITED FROM A CENTURY OF PEACE.

SO IT CAME AS A SURPRISE WHEN GULFEN, THE NATION OF ELVES, ROSE UP AND BEGAN INVADING ITS NEIGHBORS WITHOUT WARNING. WHAT WAS ONCE A PEACEFUL NATION HAD BECOME A RUTHLESS AGGRESSOR.

THE GUARDIAN COUNCIL RETALIATED, BUT THEY SEVERELY UNDERESTIMATED THE ELF KING'S POWER.

THE GREAT CITY OF CIELIS SUFFERED THE FIERCEST ATTACK DURING THE WAR. IN A BATTLE FOR THE THRONE OF ALLEDIA, THE ELVES BURNED MOST OF IT TO THE GROUND.

WHEN THE DUST CLEARED, ALL THAT WAS LEFT OF CIELIS WAS A GIANT CRATER.

MOST BELIEVE THAT THE PEOPLE OF CIELIS PERISHED IN THE FLAMES. BUT THERE ARE A FEW, LIKE THE RESISTANCE, WHO BELIEVE THE CITY STILL EXISTS INTACT.

SOME SAY THAT THE GUARDIAN COUNCIL LIFTED THE CITY OUT OF THE GROUND AND HID IT AMONG THE CLOUDS, WHERE THEY COULD SAFELY REBUILD.

OTHERS CALL IT A MYTH. BUT WE HAVE TO BELIEVE THE STORY TO BE TRUE, BECAUSE THE SURVIVAL OF ALLEDIA DEPENDS ON THE EXISTENCE OF CIELIS AND THE GUARDIAN COUNCIL.

THEY ARE OUR LAST REMAINING HOPE.

UNFORTUNATELY, HE WAS UNABLE TO COMPLETE HIS SEARCH.

IF CIELIS IS STILL AROUND, THEN WHY HASN'T THE GUARDIAN COUNCIL CONTACTED ANY OF US?

WHY HAVEN'T THEY HELPED?

THAT I DON'T KNOW.

SO IF THEY WON'T COME OUT OF HIDING TO HELP US NOW,

HOW CAN WE EXPECT THEM TO HELP US WHEN WE FIND THEM?

BECAUSE THEY WILL NEED US.

SIR --

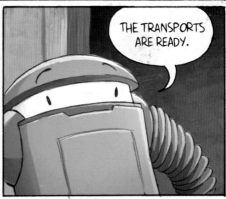

THE TRANSPORTS ARE READY.

WHEN THE TIME IS RIGHT, WE'LL COME FIND YOU.

LET'S GO, COGSLEY.

WE ARE HEADING TO A SMALL TOWN CALLED NAUTILUS, JUST EAST OF HERE.

LEON, WHERE ARE WE GOING?

ONCE THERE, WE WILL NEED TO CHARTER AN AIRSHIP TO CIELIS.

AIRSHIP?

VRRRRRN

HOLD ON TO YOUR HATS!

SO I LIKE THIS AIRSHIP PLAN.

BUT HOW WILL WE BE ABLE TO GET ONE?

WE WILL NEED TO HIRE A CAPTAIN AND CREW.

WITH WHAT? WE DON'T HAVE MONEY TO OFFER THEM.

BUT THE GUARDIAN COUNCIL DOES.

ONCE WE FIND CIELIS, MONEY WILL BE NO OBJECT.

I DON'T KNOW, LEON.

I GET THE FEELING WE WON'T HAVE TOO MANY TAKERS.

NAUTILUS IS THE SHIPPING CAPITAL OF ALLEDIA.

MOST AIRSHIPS DOCK HERE AT LEAST ONCE A YEAR.

SINCE GAINING POWER, THE ELVES HAVE FORCED PILOTS TO FLY FOR MUCH LOWER WAGES THAN THEY'RE ACCUSTOMED TO.

IT'S AN UNFORTUNATE SITUATION, BUT ONE THAT WORKS TO OUR ADVANTAGE.

THIS IS WHERE MOST OF THE PILOTS LIKE TO CONGREGATE.

WE'LL START OUR SEARCH HERE.

THE DRINKING HOLE

IS THIS A BAR?

MY CHILDREN ARE NOT GOING INTO A BAR.

IT'S NOT A BAR, MOM. IT'S A DRINKING HOLE.

YOU'RE NOT GOING IN THERE.

FINE. NAVIN CAN STAY OUT HERE WITH YOU, BUT EMILY COMES WITH ME.

COGSLEY, WATCH OVER THEM.

EMILY!

IT'S OKAY, MOM.

SO WHAT KIND OF PILOT ARE WE LOOKING FOR?

ANYONE WILLING TO TAKE THE JOB.

IT WON'T BE EASY.

WE ARE LOOKING FOR A CAPTAIN AND CREW.

WHERE ARE YOU GOING?

CIELIS.

ARE YOU KIDDING?

GET OUT OF MY FACE, SON.

WE NEED A CREW.

HAULING CARGO?

PEOPLE.

WHERE TO?

CIELIS.

HA! THE FLYING CITY!

RRRIGHT.

TAKE A HIKE.

CIELIS IS DEAD, PAL.

EVERYONE KNOWS THAT.

HEY, ENZO.

THOSE PEOPLE OVER THERE ARE LOOKING FOR THE FLYING CITY.

SHUT UP, RICO.

JOIN US AND WE CAN FIND CIELIS TOGETHER.

I HAVEN'T BEEN ABLE TO FIND THE FLYING CITY IN TEN YEARS OF SEARCHING!

WHAT MAKES YOU THINK YOU'LL FARE ANY BETTER?

BECAUSE WE HAVE A MAP.

IT'S INCOMPLETE BUT I THINK IT CAN LEAD US TO THE CITY'S LOCATION.

THESE ARE THE NOTES OF SILAS CHARNON.

HE WAS A STONEKEEPER AND FORMER MEMBER OF THE GUARDIAN COUNCIL.

HE DIED BEFORE COMPLETING HIS GUIDE.

HMM.

IT SAYS HERE THAT WITHOUT A STONEKEEPER, YOU WON'T GAIN PASSAGE TO THE CITY.

SEEING AS YOUR FRIEND IS DEAD, THIS BOOK IS NOW USELESS.

I CAN GUIDE US.

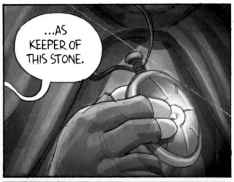

...AS KEEPER OF THIS STONE.

YOU?

WHO ARE YOU?

SILAS WAS MY GREAT-GRANDFATHER AND I HAVE TAKEN HIS PLACE...

HMPH.

THE FATE OF ALLEDIA RESTS ON HER SHOULDERS AND I MUST GET HER TO CIELIS AT ALL COSTS.

I WILL GIVE MY LIFE TO COMPLETE THIS MISSION.

LOOK, YOU'RE ASKING THE WRONG CAT.

I HAVE OTHER CLIENTS WAITING.

PLEASE, CAPTAIN.

SORRY, KID.

IT LOOKS LIKE YOU'RE IN OVER YOUR HEAD, AND I CAN'T HELP YOU.

SLAM!

HEY, YOU. TURN AND FACE ME.

DID YOU HEAR ME?

I SAID --

WE FOUND THEM!

WE FOUND THEM HIDING IN THE BACK ALLEY, ASLEEP.

PRINCE TRELLIS, I KNOW YOU HAVE ALWAYS HAD A REBELLIOUS NATURE.

BUT WHAT HAVE YOU DONE TO DESERVE THIS?

WHAT ACT OF TREASON COMPELS YOUR FATHER TO HAVE US KILL YOU?

WHAT HAVE YOU DONE?

IT'S SIMPLE.

HE'S NOT MY FATHER.

YOUR KING IS DEAD!

SZRAK!!

AGH!

40

WE HAVE TO DO SOMETHING.

I DON'T THINK WE'LL HAVE TO.

IF WE STAY QUIET, THEY MIGHT JUST GO AWAY.

THAT'S NOT WHAT I MEAN, MISKIT.

WE HAVE TO HELP THEM.

HELP THEM?!

ARE YOU CRAZY?!

THAT'S THE ELF PRINCE, MISS EMILY! HE TRIED TO KILL YOU!

HE ASKED ME TO HELP HIM DEFEAT HIS FATHER.

I JUST DIDN'T KNOW WHO HIS FATHER WAS.

EMILY, STAY PUT.

DO NOT JEOPARDIZE OUR MISSION.

I FEEL THAT BY NOT HELPING HIM, WE ARE JEOPARDIZING OUR MISSION.

I DISAGREE WITH YOUR ASSESSMENT,

BUT YOU SHOULD ALWAYS DO WHAT YOU FEEL IS RIGHT.

WAIT, WHAT?!

NO!!

KEEP YOUR HEAD DOWN, MISKIT.

MISS EMILY!

HEY!

LEAVE HIM ALONE.

WELCOME BACK, YOUNG MASTER.

I WAS BEGINNING TO THINK YOU WERE GOING TO IGNORE ME FOR GOOD.

CAPTAIN, WE'RE GOING TO NEED YOUR HELP.

AND WE DON'T HAVE MUCH TIME.

YES, OF COURSE.

OUR SHIP IS AT THE DOCK.

MISKIT, GET EVERYONE INTO THE TRANSPORT.

EVERYONE?

WHAT ABOUT THEM?

YES.

BRING THEM, TOO.

NOW HURRY AND GET EVERY-ONE OUTSIDE!

FSSHT!
CLANK!

THIS IS E-MEK FIVE, APPROACHING THE TARGET.

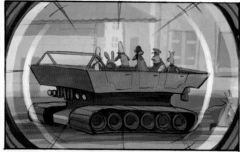

I HAVE THE ENEMY IN MY SIGHTS!

EMILY, ARE YOU OKAY?

EVERYBODY GET IN!

WE HAVE TO GET MOVING NOW!

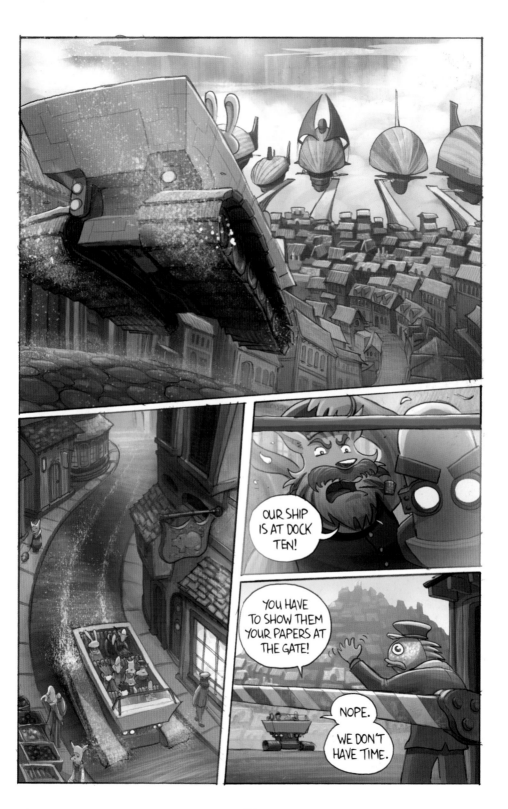

THIS THING IS A PIECE OF JUNK!

AND IT'S THE TINIEST SHIP HERE!

SHE MIGHT BE SMALL, BUT SHE'S FAST.

HMPH.

EVERYBODY GET ABOARD QUICKLY!

TARGET ONE DESTROYED!

ACQUIRING NEW TARGET!

GET US OUT OF HERE NOW!!!

PUT PUT

VRRRRR

SZRAK!!!

WE HAVE TO FIND A WAY HOME!

IF WE STAY HERE, WE'RE GOING TO GET SERIOUSLY HURT.

OR WORSE.

I TOLD YOU, MOM.

IF YOU GO HOME, I CAN'T COME WITH YOU.

BUT WHY NOT?!

WHAT'S HOLDING YOU BACK?

IT IS THE CURSE OF THE STONEKEEPER.

THE STONE WILL NOT LET YOU LEAVE NOW, WILL IT?

NO. IT WON'T.

A CURSE?

THAT'S ENOUGH, LUGER.

DO NOT SPEAK WITH THEM.

THEY ALREADY KNOW TOO MUCH.

MY DAUGHTER SAVED YOUR LIFE, AND THIS IS HOW YOU TREAT HER?!

SHE SHOULD HAVE LEFT US ALONE.

DON'T MIND HIM.

WE ARE GRATEFUL FOR YOUR DAUGHTER'S ACTIONS.

HEAR THAT?

YOU SHOULD BE MORE LIKE YOUR FATHER.

TRELLIS.

HMPH.

SHUT.

I'M SORRY YOU HAVE TO DEAL WITH THAT.

YOU MUST UNDERSTAND,

HE IS NOT MY SON.

TRELLIS.

YOU SAID YOU WANTED MY HELP IN DEFEATING YOUR FATHER, THE ELF KING.

WHY TURN AGAINST HIM?

IT WAS A MISTAKE TO INVOLVE YOU IN THIS.

GO BACK BEFORE IT'S TOO LATE.

THIS MIGHT BE OUR LAST NIGHT ALIVE, WALRIG.

SO DRINK UP!

WE NEED ANOTHER ROUND, SHORTY!

AND PUT IT ON THE ELF KING'S TAB!

GULP!

IF I HELP YOU FIND THEM, YOU'LL GET YOUR BOUNTY AND WE'LL BE EXECUTED FOR FAILING THE KING'S ORDERS.

NOT A GOOD DEAL FOR US.

YOU'RE ON YOUR OWN HERE, BUDDY.

I ALWAYS HAVE BEEN.

KCHUNK!

SPATCH!

MMF!

THIS IS A MEMORY EXTRACTOR.

I PULL THIS TRIGGER AND I STEAL ALL YOUR MEMORIES.

IT WILL TAKE YEARS TO RECOVER FROM IT.

NOW LET'S SEE WHAT'S HIDING IN THAT PEA BRAIN OF YOURS.

HMM.

YOU. WHO ARE THESE PEOPLE?

THEIR NAMES ARE ENZO AND RICO. THEY ARE THE CREW OF THE LUNA MOTH.

DO YOU KNOW WHERE THEY MIGHT BE HEADED?

I HEARD THEM SAY THEY WERE LOOKING FOR CIELIS.

CIELIS?

I THOUGHT IT HAD BEEN DESTROYED.

MOST PEOPLE BELIEVE IT IS LONG GONE,

BUT SOME, LIKE ENZO, BELIEVE IT IS HIDDEN IN THE CLOUDS.

CIELIS WAS THE CITY OF STONEKEEPERS, RIGHT?

YES, SIR.

SO THE FUGITIVE SCUM MUST BE AFTER REINFORCEMENTS.

VERY INTERESTING.

FOR YOUR TROUBLES.

THANK YOU, SIR.

FLING!

WHOSE SIDE ARE YOU ON, GABILAN?

COME AGAIN?

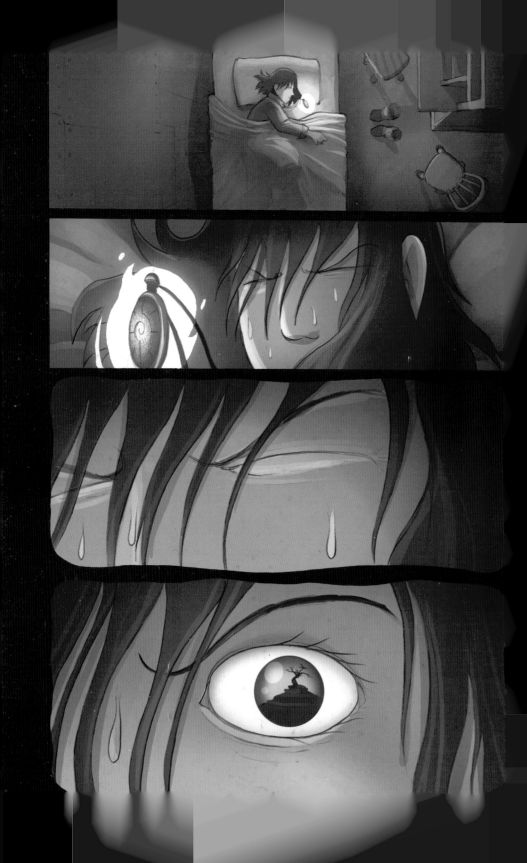

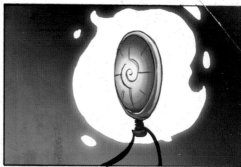

THAT'S THE GOLBEZ CYCLE.

IT'S A MASSIVE STORM SYSTEM.

CAN WE FLY THROUGH IT?

THE *MOTH* WASN'T DESIGNED TO HANDLE SUCH STRONG WEATHER.

ARE YOU CERTAIN THIS IS THE CITY'S LOCATION?

IT IS THE FINAL LOCATION IN SILAS'S GUIDE.

IT'S WHERE SILAS LEFT OFF BEFORE HE PASSED AWAY.

ALL SIGNS POINT DIRECTLY TO THE EYE OF THE STORM.

DO YOU KNOW WHAT YOU'RE ASKING ME TO DO?

THE GOLBEZ CYCLE HAS BEEN RAGING ON FOR CENTURIES WITH NO INDICATION OF SLOWING.

THE STORM IS MANAGEABLE ON CERTAIN ROUTES,

BUT THE AREA IS A KNOWN GRAVEYARD FOR AIRSHIPS. MOST CAPTAINS ARE ADVISED TO STAY WELL CLEAR OF THE TERRITORY.

I CAN FLY US INTO THE STORM,

BUT I NEED TO KNOW FOR CERTAIN THAT CIELIS WILL BE THERE WAITING FOR US. THE RISKS ARE TOO HUGE.

I CAN'T GUARANTEE THAT CIELIS IS THERE, BUT THIS GUIDE IS THE BEST LEAD WE HAVE.

ANOTHER LEAP OF FAITH?

YOU KNOW I'M STILL WITH YOU ON THIS, CHIEF.

BUT I'M STARTING TO FEEL LIKE WE'RE DRIFTING UP A CREEK WITHOUT A PADDLE.

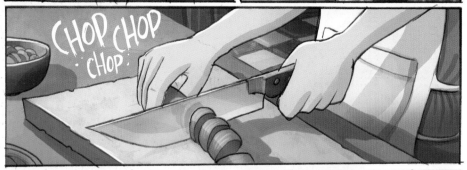

CHOP CHOP CHOP

HOW ARE THOSE CARROTS?

CHOP CHOP

ALMOST DONE.

JUST KEEP STIRRING?

YES. YES.

DON'T LET IT BURN.

WE'RE GOING TO BEGIN OUR DAY CLEANING THE SHIP.

I WANT EACH OF YOU TO PICK A SPOT OF FLOOR AND CLEAN IT AS IF YOU HAVE TO EAT OFF IT.

NOW HOP TO IT, PORK CHOPS!

EMILY,

YOU HAVE SHOWN THAT YOU ARE SKILLED AT USING THE STONE MAGIC TO ATTACK.

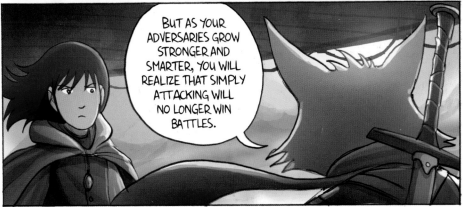

BUT AS YOUR ADVERSARIES GROW STRONGER AND SMARTER, YOU WILL REALIZE THAT SIMPLY ATTACKING WILL NO LONGER WIN BATTLES.

IT IS LIKELY THAT IT WILL NOT BE YOUR ABILITY TO ATTACK, BUT TO DEFEND, THAT WILL BE THE KEY TO VICTORY.

DEFEND?

YOUR STONE MAGIC IS AS VERSATILE AS YOUR IMAGINATION.

IT CAN BECOME A DEVASTATING WEAPON, OR IT CAN BE A HIGHLY EFFECTIVE SHIELD.

DO YOU REMEMBER WHAT YOU LEARNED AT DEMON'S HEAD?

THE ABILITY TO HOLD SOMETHING WITHOUT DESTROYING IT.

NOW YOU WILL NEED TO TAKE IT A STEP FURTHER.

I WANT YOU TO LIFT THIS BOTTLE.

GOOD.

NOW PROTECT IT.

LATCH!

SHING!

YOU'RE TOO FAST!

IS THAT WHAT YOU'LL TELL YOUR ENEMIES?

YOUR MAGIC IS OFTEN TRIGGERED BY YOUR EMOTIONS, AND THAT CAN BE DANGEROUS.

DEFENSE REQUIRES A MORE CALCULATED APPROACH.

YOU MUST STAY CALM, COOL, AND COLLECTED AT ALL TIMES.

NOW TRY AGAIN.

I'M READY.

AREN'T YOU GOING TO ATTACK?

MOST ENEMIES WILL STRIKE WHEN YOU LEAST EXPECT IT.

SO YOU MUST BE AWARE AT ALL TIMES --

-- EVEN WHEN YOUR GUARD IS DOWN.

WITH PRACTICE, YOUR AWARENESS WILL GROW.

AS WILL YOUR PATIENCE.

SHING!

DON'T LET YOUR FRUSTRATION GET TO YOU.

READY TO TRY AGAIN?

SWEEP SWEEP

WHAT ABOUT MISKIT?

HE'S --

IGNORE HIM.

WORK PAST THE DISTRACTIONS.

TOSS!

GOTO FARMS
CAVAS APPLE TEA

BUT LUGER SAYS IT'S LUNCHTIME.

POTATO SALAD?

I EAT OIL.

THIS IS REALLY GOOD.

WHERE DID YOU LEARN TO COOK LIKE THIS?

HONESTLY, I CAN'T REMEMBER.

IN FACT, THERE IS VERY LITTLE ABOUT MY LIFE I CAN REMEMBER.

WHAT I WANT TO KNOW IS WHY YOU TWO WERE CONSIDERED FUGITIVES.

YOU BOYS DO SOMETHING WE SHOULD BE WORRIED ABOUT?

IT'S NOT YOUR BUSINESS.

EVERYTHING ON THIS SHIP IS MY BUSINESS, SON.

NOW WHAT DID YOU DO TO GET ON YOUR DADDY'S BAD SIDE?

HE IS NOT MY FATHER, CAPTAIN.

HE ISN'T WHAT YOU THINK HE IS.

TRELLIS, YOU DIDN'T FINISH YOUR FOOD.

JUST LEAVE HIM BE.

THEY GET LIKE THAT AT THIS AGE.

SPAK!

NICE WORK, EMILY.

THIS WEARS ME OUT FASTER THAN OFFENSIVE MAGIC.

YOU'LL GET USED TO IT.

WITH PRACTICE, ANYTHING CAN BECOME SECOND NATURE.

HEY!

Z SNRK! HUH?! OH!

WHATEVER HAPPENED TO 'ONLY AS STRONG AS OUR WEAKEST LINK'?

STOP GIVING ME A HARD TIME, KID.

I WAS JUST MAKING SURE THIS HAT WAS CLEAN.

RIGHT.

SO IS THIS THE AUTO-PILOT?

MEEP MEEP!

YEAH.

SAMSON COST ME AN ARM AND A LEG, BUT HE'S WORTH IT.

TRADED A WHOLE ENGINE TO GET HIM.

CAN I TRY FLYING THE SHIP?

I'VE FLOWN A PLANE BEFORE.

NO WAY, KID.

THIS IS A COMPLICATED PIECE OF EQUIPMENT.

SAMSON HERE IS HIGHLY TRAINED.

IT DOESN'T LOOK VERY DIFFICULT.

LOOK, KID, YOU DON'T BELONG UP HERE.

BUT IF YOU DO A GOOD JOB CLEANING, I'LL CONSIDER LETTING YOU STEER FOR A FEW MINUTES.

WHOOOSH!!!

NOW GET BACK THERE AND --

WYVERNS.

WHAT'S A WYVERN?

JUST DO AS I SAY!

HEY, MOM.

THE CAPTAIN SAYS TO GET INSIDE.

HOLD ON, NAVIN.

I'M ALMOST DONE.

MOM, I THINK IT'S SERIOUS.

WHAT'S THE MATTER?

IT'S AN EARWIG OR SOMETHING.

WHATEVER IT IS, IT'S HUGE.

DID YOU SEE THAT?

DING! DING! DING! DI

SOMETHING'S WRONG.

EVERYBODY INSIDE!

DING DIN

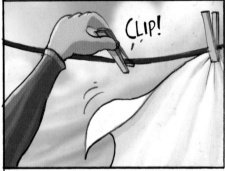

CLIP!

OKAY, THAT WAS THE LAST ONE.

SWOOP!

WHAT THE --

EMILY?!

SHWIP!!

WHAT WERE YOU DOING?!

I WAS TRYING TO PROTECT HER!

PROTECT HER FROM WHAT?!

FROM THAT.

SKREEE!!

IT'S BEEN A WHILE SINCE THE LAST WYVERN ATTACK, ENZO.

WHAT IF THE STUNNER DOESN'T WORK ANYMORE?

WHIRRRR KCHUNK! CHUNK

UNFORTUNATELY, WE DON'T HAVE OTHER OPTIONS, RICO.

WHAT ARE THEY AFTER?

THEY'RE ON THE HUNT FOR FOOD.

BUT THEY'RE USUALLY NOT SO AGGRESSIVE.

WHATEVER IT IS THEY WANT, WE BETTER LET THEM KNOW TO LOOK ELSE-WHERE!

KPOOF!

I DON'T THINK THOSE TOYS ARE GOING TO DO IT, CAPTAIN.

CRUNCH!

KRNK!

HE'S TEARING THE ENGINE APART!

SZRAK!! SPAK!

IF THAT ENGINE GOES DOWN, WE'LL BE STUCK GOING AROUND IN CIRCLES.

HERE, TIE THIS AROUND YOUR WAIST.

WHAT ARE YOU DOING?

I'M GOING TO GO OUT THERE AND FIX IT.

WE HAVE TO GET CLEAR OF THESE CLOUDS.

IT'S THESE THUNDERHEADS.

WYVERNS LIKE TO FLY THROUGH THEM.

SPAK!

BZT!

CLAMP!

SPAK!!

I CAN FIX THIS!

LOOK OUT! WE'VE GOT COMPANY!

EVERYBODY GET INSIDE!

HURRY!

ARE YOU ALL RIGHT?

YOU'RE DRENCHED IN SWEAT!

I'M FINE, MOM.

EEP!

AGH!

HELP!!

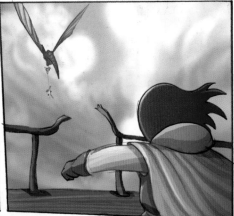

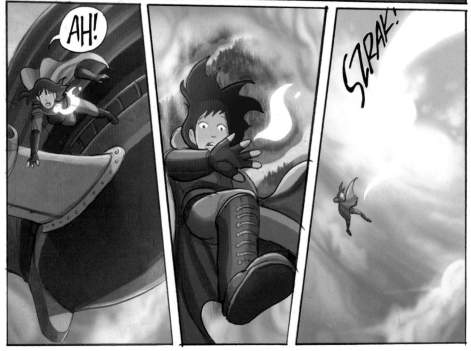

WHAT WERE YOU THINKING?

WE HAVE TO GO BACK.

WE CAN'T LEAVE THEM BEHIND!

STOP THE SHIP! WE HAVE TO TURN AROUND!

ARE YOU CRAZY?!

WE HAVE TO GET OUT OF THESE CLOUDS BEFORE THE WYVERNS TEAR US APART!

BUT WE LOST MISKIT AND COGSLEY!

WHAT?!

A WYVERN TOOK THEM.

I'M SORRY, KID, BUT THERE'S NOTHING WE CAN DO.

THEY'RE TOO FAST FOR THIS SHIP.

EVEN IF WE CHASED AFTER YOUR FRIENDS, WE WOULD NEVER CATCH UP.

I'M SORRY.

LEON, YOU HAVE TO CONVINCE THEM TO TURN AROUND!

I'M AFRAID ENZO'S RIGHT, EMILY.

THERE IS NOTHING WE CAN DO.

WE CAN'T JUST LEAVE THEM BEHIND!

THEIR JOB WAS TO PROTECT YOU.

NOT THE OTHER WAY AROUND.

PUTTING YOU IN HARM'S WAY TO SAVE THEM IS THE LAST THING SILAS WOULD HAVE WANTED.

IT'S NOT YOUR FAULT, EMILY.

YOU KNOW THAT'S NOT TRUE.

WE NEED TO REFUEL SOON, ENZO.

WE ALSO NEED TO REPAIR THE ENGINE.

✷SIGH✷

WHAT'S THE MATTER?

THERE'S ONLY ONE FUELING STATION SERVICING THIS ROUTE.

AND I WAS HOPING WE COULD AVOID A PIT STOP.

UH-OH.

ARE WE WHERE I THINK WE ARE?

SHE'S THE ONLY ONE OUT HERE, RICO.

LET'S JUST HOPE OLD WOUNDS HEAL FAST.

TELL ME SOMETHING I DON'T KNOW, RICO.

I'M NOT GOING TO LIKE THIS ANY MORE THAN SHE WILL.

SHE'S NOT GOING TO LIKE THIS, ENZO.

I JUST NEED FUEL, SELINA.

AND I'LL BE OUT OF YOUR HAIR.

I THOUGHT YOU STOPPED SAILING THIS ROUTE LONG AGO.

I DID.

ARE YOU OKAY, CAPTAIN?

YEAH, I'M FINE.

I'D LIKE YOU ALL TO MEET SOMEONE.

THIS IS SELINA FIGGINS.

SHE IS THE OWNER OF THIS FUELING STATION.

ARE YOU STILL CHASING THAT STUPID FLYING CITY?

FOR YOUR INFORMATION, THESE PEOPLE HAVE ASKED ME TO TAKE THEM THERE.

THEY SEEM VERY CAPABLE, AND I'M CERTAIN THEY WEREN'T EATEN.

DON'T WORRY, NAVIN.

I'M SURE THEY'RE OKAY.

THIS IS LIKE WHEN YOU LOSE YOUR TOYS.

THEY'LL TURN UP AGAIN, EVENTUALLY.

I DUNNO, MOM.

I DON'T THINK THIS IS LIKE THAT AT ALL.

WE CAN'T INVITE TROUBLE LIKE THIS, ENZO.

YOU SHOULD HAVE WARNED US.

HEY, I WAS TRYING TO AVOID THIS PLACE.

AND IF IT'S SELINA YOU'RE WORRIED ABOUT, DON'T SWEAT IT.

SHE WOULDN'T SELL US OUT TO THE ELVES.

SHE MAY HATE MY GUTS, BUT I TRUST HER.

I DON'T CARE IF YOU TRUST HER.

WE JUST HAVE TO MAKE SURE WE DON'T ATTRACT UNWANTED ATTENTION.

ONE FALSE MOVE CAN JEOPARDIZE OUR ENTIRE MISSION.

SLURRRP...

YOU SHOULD HAVE LET ME HELP YOU.

I DON'T WANT YOU NEAR MY FAMILY.

YOU DON'T TRUST ME.

I GET THE IMPRESSION THE FEELING IS MUTUAL.

FAIR ENOUGH.

BUT THE NEXT TIME I TRY TO HELP, I SUGGEST YOU STAY OUT OF MY WAY.

FOR YOUR SAKE.

WAIT.

YOU NEVER ANSWERED MY QUESTION.

WHY TURN AGAINST YOUR FATHER?

IT'S A PRIVATE MATTER.

IF YOU WANT ME TO TRUST YOU, THEN YOU NEED TO START TRUSTING ME.

AND YOU CAN BEGIN BY TELLING ME WHY YOU NEED MY HELP IN TAKING DOWN YOUR FATHER.

ON GONDOA MOUNTAIN, THE DAY WE MET.

THE ARACHNOPOD CARRYING YOUR MOTHER WAS SUPPOSED TO FIND ITS WAY BACK TO THE ELF KING, BUT I STOPPED IT.

IT WAS SEEN AS AN ACT OF TREASON.

MY FATHER WAS LOOKING FOR A YOUNG STONEKEEPER TO TAKE MY PLACE AS HIS SUCCESSOR, AND I WANTED TO STOP HIM.

I WANTED TO USE YOU AGAINST HIM, BUT I FAILED.

HE WANTED ME TO BE HIS SUCCESSOR?

BEING JEALOUS, I ASSUMED THAT WAS HIS WISH.

BUT I'M AFRAID THE TRUTH IS FAR MORE SINISTER.

FOR THE PAST SEVERAL YEARS, I HAVE HAD TROUBLE REMEMBERING THINGS. THE KINDS OF THINGS ONE DOESN'T FORGET.

MUCH OF MY CHILDHOOD AND EARLY LIFE WERE A BLANK SLATE, AND I SUSPECTED MY FATHER HAD SOMETHING TO DO WITH IT.

STRANGELY ENOUGH, ONE OF THE FEW REMAINING IMAGES IN MY MEMORY WAS THAT OF MY FATHER'S FACE. IT WAS THE ONLY THING I SAW CLEARLY, AS IF I HAD DECIDED IT WAS THE ONLY MEMORY WORTH KEEPING.

I WANTED TO SEE HIM AGAIN, TO CATCH A GLIMPSE OF HIS FACE BEHIND THE MASK, WITH THE HOPE THAT IT MIGHT HELP BRING BACK MORE MEMORIES.

UNDER THE COVER OF NIGHT, I SNUCK INTO HIS TOWER AND BEDROOM CHAMBER.

AND WHAT I SAW I WILL NEVER FORGET.

BEHIND THE MASK WAS MY FATHER'S FACE, JUST AS I HAD REMEMBERED IT.

BUT JUST AS MY MEMORY WAS FROZEN IN TIME, THE FACE BEFORE ME WAS FROZEN AS WELL.

SOMETHING WAS WRONG.

HIS FEATURES WERE GAUNT AND GRAY, WITH SKIN LIKE STONE. HIS EYES GLAZED OVER BY A MILKY WHITE SUBSTANCE, AND NOTHING BUT A COLD EMPTINESS BEHIND THEM.

HE WAS DEAD.

THE ELF KING IS NOTHING MORE THAN A WALKING CORPSE, AND WHATEVER LIVES INSIDE OF IT KILLED MY FATHER.

I WANT TO DESTROY IT BEFORE IT DOES MORE HARM TO THE NATION OF ELVES.

IF HE'S DEAD, THEN HOW CAN YOU DEFEAT HIM? HOW CAN ANYONE KILL HIM?

YOU MUST DESTROY THE STONE.

A STONEKEEPER PROVIDES BOTH FOCUS AND BALANCE FOR THE STONE'S POWER.

A STONE IS NOT KNOWN TO SURVIVE WITHOUT A KEEPER.

BUT THIS ONE HAS FOUND A WAY TO REANIMATE THE BODY OF ITS DEAD MASTER,

USING THE DARKEST KIND OF MAGIC THERE IS.

AND IT IS LIKELY THAT THE KING WAS NOT THE FIRST VICTIM.

HAVING TROUBLE SLEEPING?

I NOTICED YOU WEREN'T IN BED.

CAN I JOIN YOU?

YOU SHOULD BE SLEEPING, MOM.

WE HAVE A LONG DAY TOMORROW.

DON'T WORRY ABOUT ME.

WHEN YOU AND NAVIN WERE BORN, I GOT USED TO OPERATING WITHOUT SLEEP.

I'LL MANAGE.

NOW TELL ME WHY WE'RE BOTH STILL AWAKE.

I JUST HAD A BAD DREAM.

EXCEPT I'M NOT SURE IT WAS JUST A DREAM.

I KNOW EXACTLY WHAT YOU MEAN.

YOU DO?

WHEN YOUR FATHER PASSED AWAY, I FELT PRETTY MUCH LIKE YOU DO NOW.

I HAD MORE WEIGHT ON MY SHOULDERS THAN I COULD HANDLE.

WITHOUT HIS SUPPORT, I DIDN'T KNOW WHAT TO DO. I FELT SO ALONE.

BUT WHEN I LOOKED AT YOUR FACES, I REALIZED I HAD TO STOP FEELING BAD FOR MYSELF.

I HAD TO FOCUS ON TAKING GOOD CARE OF YOU, AND THERE JUST WASN'T TIME TO DWELL ON IT.

SO I TRUSTED MYSELF TO FIGURE IT OUT.

AND MY WORRIES VANISHED.

IF YOU CAN FIND THE CONFIDENCE TO TRUST YOURSELF,

YOU CAN MAKE IT THROUGH ANY SITUATION, NO MATTER HOW BAD THINGS MAY SEEM.

NOW STOP WORRYING SO MUCH.

YOU'RE WASTING YOUR TIME.

COME HERE.

YOU'RE NOT WORRIED?

I'M YOUR MOTHER, SWEETIE.

WORRYING ABOUT YOU IS MY FULL-TIME JOB.

IT'S TIME YOU STARTED THINKING ABOUT SETTLING DOWN.

YOU'RE GETTING OLD, YOU KNOW?

I'VE STILL GOT QUITE A FEW YEARS LEFT, AND I INTEND TO USE THEM TO REALIZE MY DREAMS.

SOMEDAY YOU'LL HAVE TO STOP CHASING THESE RAINBOWS AND THINK ABOUT WHAT FUTURE YOU HAVE LEFT.

THIS ISN'T A RAINBOW.

LOOK,

JUST REMEMBER THAT WHEN YOU DECIDE TO SETTLE DOWN, THERE WILL BE A JOB WAITING FOR YOU HERE AT THE STATION.

THANKS FOR THE OFFER, SEL, BUT I PLAN TO SETTLE DOWN ON A CITY HIGH ABOVE THE CLOUDS.

I'LL SEND YOU A POSTCARD.

VRRRR

IF WE TRAVEL THROUGH THE LIGHTER AREAS OF THE STORM, WE MAY BE ABLE TO SEE CIELIS FROM AFAR.

I'LL TAKE US ALL THE WAY IN.

WE'RE STILL NOT SURE CIELIS IS THERE.

THERE'S REALLY ONLY ONE WAY TO FIND OUT FOR SURE. RIGHT, CHIEF?

WE BETTER LET THE OTHERS KNOW TO BUCKLE UP.

I GET THE FEELING WE'RE NOT THE ONLY ONES OUT HERE.

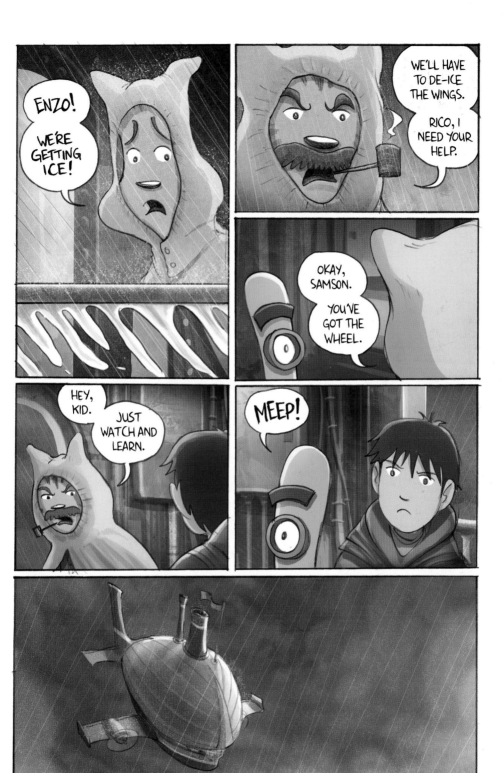

WAIT UNTIL I GIVE THE WORD!

NOW, RICO! FULL BLAST!

SPSHHH!

ENZO! WE'VE GOT A PROBLEM!

FUNNEL CLOUDS!

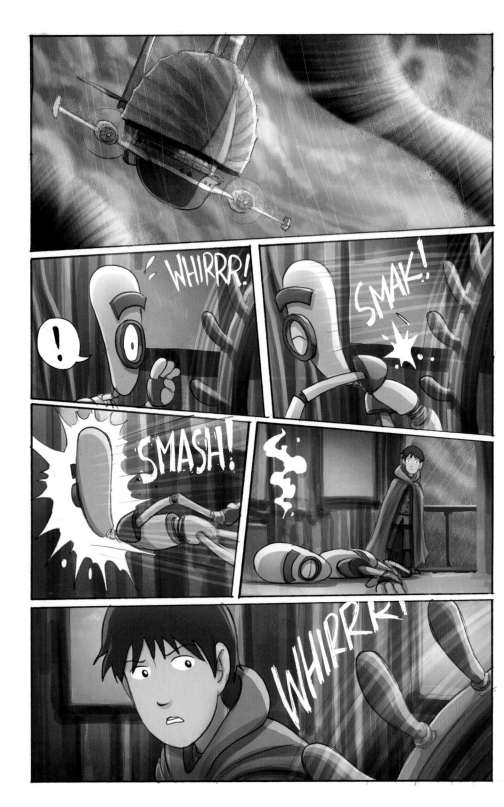

WAY TO GO, SAMSON! THAT WAS SOME PRETTY FANCY FLYING.

HMM.

YOU CAN TAKE OVER IF YOU WANT.

LOOKS LIKE YOU HAVE IT UNDER CONTROL.

CARRY ON.

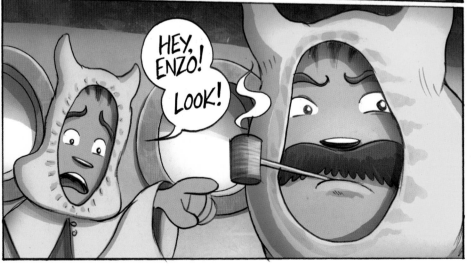

IS THAT CIELIS?

NO.

IT CAN'T BE.

TRUTHFULLY, I'M NOT SURE WHAT THAT IS...

ACCORDING TO THE BOOK, THIS ISLAND IS SOME SORT OF BEACON.

THIS PUZZLE MUST HAVE BEEN PLACED HERE TO TEST THOSE SEEKING PASSAGE TO THE CITY.

HOW IS ALL OF THIS SUSPENDED IN THE AIR?

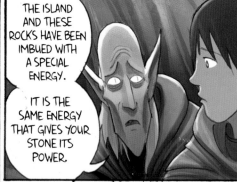

THE ISLAND AND THESE ROCKS HAVE BEEN IMBUED WITH A SPECIAL ENERGY.

IT IS THE SAME ENERGY THAT GIVES YOUR STONE ITS POWER.

EMILY.

TRELLIS.

LET'S BEGIN.

CHOP CHOP CHOP

WHY DO I ALWAYS GET KITCHEN DUTY?

I CAN'T EVEN COOK!

SIZZLE

C'MON, RICO.

WE ALL NEED TO EAT BEFORE GOING TO CIELIS.

THIS IS JUST AS IMPORTANT AS WHAT THEY'RE DOING.

HOLD STILL.

PUT YOUR HANDS UP WHERE I CAN SEE THEM.

SPANG!

RICO! WARN THE OTHERS!

BAM!

SLUMP!

NO!

166

SLAM!

LET GO OF ME!

I DON'T WANT TO HURT YOU.

I SIMPLY WANT TO JOIN YOUR LITTLE PARTY.

AND I WILL NEED YOUR HELP.

VERY GOOD.

NOW GUIDE THE PIECES TOGETHER.

ONE LAST PIECE.

PLINK!

FWOOOM!

PERSONALLY, I'M MORE THAN A LITTLE CURIOUS TO SEE THE RESULTS.

THAT VOICE...

I KNOW THAT VOICE.

I HAVE INFORMED THE ELF KING ABOUT THE LOCATION OF THIS BEACON TEMPLE, SO IT IS ONLY A MATTER OF TIME BEFORE THE FORCES OF GULFEN RAVAGE CIELIS ONCE AGAIN.

HOW DOES IT FEEL TO BE RESPONSIBLE FOR THE DEMISE OF THE GUARDIAN COUNCIL?

EMILY, I CAN GET YOU MAYBE TEN SECONDS.

WHAT?

I CAN PROTECT YOUR MOTHER FOR A BRIEF MOMENT, LEAVING HIM OPEN FOR AN ATTACK.

YOU'LL HAVE ENOUGH TIME TO STRIKE HIM DOWN.

YOU'RE THE ONE WHO DID THIS TO ME!

YOU'RE THE ONE WHO MADE ME FORGET EVERYTHING!

I WAS ONLY FOLLOWING YOUR FATHER'S ORDERS, LUGER.

MY FATHER?

FATHER?

LUGER'S YOUR BROTHER?

OH, LUGER, YOU DIDN'T KNOW?

I MUST HAVE DONE A BETTER JOB THAN I REALIZED.

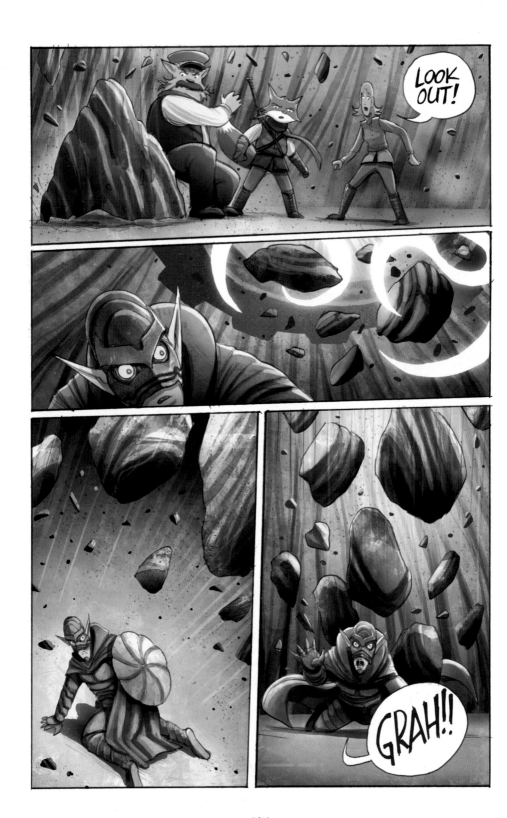

THE STONE
HAS ITS OWN
AGENDA.

AND WHEN
IT'S FINISHED
WITH YOU...

YOU THINK
YOU'RE IN
CONTROL.

BUT YOU'RE
NOT.

...YOU
WILL DIE
LIKE THE
REST.

EMILY!

MOM!

DUNCAN, RELEASE THEM.

AND THE ELVES?

TELL YOUR MEN TO LET THEM GO! THEY'RE WITH ME!

YOU HEARD THE LADY.

BUT, SIR, YOU CAN'T BE SERIOUS!

THIS STONE-KEEPER MAY VERY WELL BE A NEW MEMBER OF THE COUNCIL.

I WANT YOU TO TREAT HER ORDERS AS IF THEY WERE MY OWN.

YES, SIR.

NOW THIS ISN'T JUST A FREE PASS, OLD MAN.

UNDERSTAND THAT I WILL BE WATCHING OVER THE BOTH OF YOU LIKE A HAWK.

AND YOU MUST BE THE SOLDIER, LEON REDBEARD.

YES, SIR.

FUNNY.

THE REPORT DIDN'T INDICATE YOU WERE A FOX.

THAT MUST MEAN YOU HAVE MY BIRTH RECORDS.

THIS CURSE TOOK HOLD DURING MY CHILDHOOD.

WELL, THE GUARDIAN COUNCIL THANKS YOU FOR BRINGING EMILY HERE SAFELY.

I WILL TAKE OVER FROM HERE.

DUNCAN, GATHER EVERYONE AND ESCORT THEM TO THE SHIP.

WE LEAVE IMMEDIATELY.

YES, SIR.

THE ELF KING KNOWS WHERE THIS PLACE IS LOCATED.

THEY'RE PROBABLY ON THEIR WAY.

WE KNOW.

SHE WAS NEVER MEANT TO BE TOWED.

HEY! BE CAREFUL!

THEY WILL TEACH YOU THINGS THAT I CANNOT.

EMILY!

MAX HERE HAS BEEN TELLING ME ALL ABOUT THE SCHOOL.

I THINK IT'S EXCITING!

SCHOOL?

IT IS WHY YOU'RE HERE, ISN'T IT?

WHY WE'RE BOTH HERE.

WE WILL BE TRAINED AND TESTED TO SEE WHO AMONG US WILL MAKE UP THE NEW GUARDIAN COUNCIL.

WE'LL BE ENTERING THE JUMP GATE MOMENTARILY.

THANK YOU, DUNCAN.

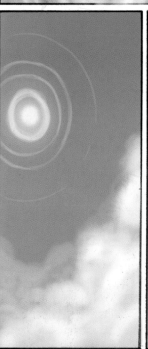

WELCOME TO YOUR NEW HOME, EMILY.

RICO, FIND A CAMERA AND DOCUMENT THIS MOMENT...

END OF BOOK THREE

Written and Illustrated by
KAZU KIBUISHI

Lead Production Assistant
JASON CAFFOE

Colors by
Jason Caffoe
Kazu Kibuishi

Color Assistance by
Anthony Wu
Michael Regina
Denver Jackson
Amy Kim Kibuishi

Color Flatting by
Denver Jackson
Jason Caffoe
Michael Regina
Stuart Livingston
Ryan Hoffman
Anthony Wu

Special Thanks

Judy Hansen, David Saylor, Cassandra Pelham, Phil Falco, Gordon Luk, Ben Zhu & the Gallery Nucleus crew, Nick & Melissa Harris, the Flight artists, JP Ahonen, Tony Cliff, Richard Pose, Rachel Ormiston, Tim Ganter, Taka Kibuishi, Nancy Caffoe, June Kibuishi & Sunni Kim

ABOUT THE AUTHOR

Kazu Kibuishi is the creator of the #1 *New York Times* bestselling Amulet series. *Amulet, Book One: The Stonekeeper* was an ALA Best Book for Young Adults and a Children's Choice Book Award finalist. He is also the creator of *Copper*, a collection of his popular webcomic that features an adventuresome boy-and-dog pair. Kazu also illustrated the covers of the 15th anniversary paperback editions of the Harry Potter series written by J. K. Rowling. He lives and works in Seattle, Washington, with his wife, Amy Kim Kibuishi, and their children.

Visit Kazu online at www.boltcity.com.

GULFEN
GANON'S GATE
Stengard
Valcor
Frontera
Sparkton
Lucien
Golbez
Cycle
PIT ROCK
Junivale
The Spires
Selina's
station
N
W
E
S
Coco
Ippo

ALSO BY
KAZU KIBUISHI

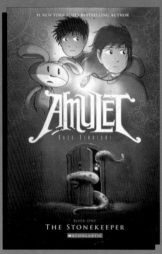
BOOK ONE
THE STONEKEEPER

BOOK TWO
THE STONEKEEPER'S CURSE

BOOK THREE
THE CLOUD SEARCHERS

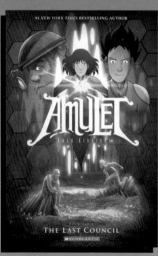
BOOK FOUR
THE LAST COUNCIL

BOOK FIVE
PRINCE OF THE ELVES

BOOK SIX
ESCAPE FROM LUCIEN